Millie

Alfie

Ben

Ruby

Jemma

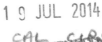

Mikey

Matt

Dylan

Sam & Arthur

Harry

Ralph

Sophie

Max

For Dylan, enjoy whatever
whizzy busy job you choose

ORCHARD BOOKS
338 Euston Road, London NW1 3BH
Orchard Books Australia
Level 17/207 Kent Street, Sydney, NSW 2000
First published in 2013 by Orchard Books
ISBN 978 1 40831 551 4
Text and illustrations © Guy Parker-Rees 2013

The right of Guy Parker-Rees to be identified as the author
and illustrator of this book has been asserted by him in accordance
with the Copyright, Designs and Patents Act, 1988.

A CIP catalogue record for this book is available from the British Library.

1 3 5 7 9 10 8 6 4 2

Printed in China

Orchard Books is a division of Hachette Children's Books,
an Hachette UK company.
www.hachette.co.uk

Tom & Millie's
WHIZZY
BUSY
PEOPLE

Guy Parker-Rees

Can you find the ladybird
on every busy page?

ORCHARD

T om and Millie are talking about what
they want to be when they grow up.
"We need to have the best job ever!" says Millie.
"We can get ideas from our family," says Tom.
"Mummy loves her job at the hospital,
let's go there first."

Tom and Millie's mummy is a nurse. She's bandaging Adam's head. Some of Tom and Millie's other friends are there, too. "Look, Noah has had an x-ray," says Millie. "And Sarah has a pan stuck on her head."
"It's busy!" gasps Tom. "Let's go to Daddy's fire station next."

It's all go at the fire station!
"Jake is pretending to drive the fire engine,"
laughs Tom. "And . . . sniff . . . it smells like Poppy's
daddy is burning the sausages again!"

"Look!" gasps Millie. "Florence is stuck
in the tree and Daddy is rescuing her!"
"He's really busy, so let's go and see
Auntie Alice at the airport," suggests Tom.

Everyone is coming and going at the airport.
"There's Auntie Alice in her big red plane,"
says Tom. "She loves being a pilot."
"And there's Toby on his purple suitcase and
Lucy with her toy helicopter," says Millie.
"Come on!" smiles Tom. "Let's go to see
Uncle Mark now."

Uncle Mark drives a green truck at the Recycling Centre.
"Lots of people are here today," says Millie. "There's
Hannah in her red bicycle buggy, and Freddie with his
orange wagon."
"Looking for the best job in the world is making
me hungry!" says Tom. "Let's go to the café."

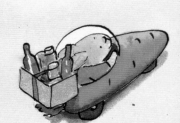

Cousins Jenny and Jim work at the café.
"What shall we have to eat?" asks Millie. "Tomato soup like Olivia, or an ice cream like Alfie?"
"I think Ben wants us to join his birthday party!" says Tom.
"Jenny is pouring the juice and Jim is taking them five pizzas."
"Yum!" says Millie. "After lunch, let's go to Auntie May's shop."

The shop is bustling with customers.
"I can see Ruby picking a pineapple and Saul pushing a mini trolley but where is Auntie May?" asks Tom.
"There she is," says Millie. "She's working at the till."
"Oh, she looks busy," sighs Tom. "And – oops! – Jemma just dropped a jar of jam."
"Time for us to go," says Millie.
"Let's visit Uncle Ed."

"We always spot our friends at the museum,"
says Millie. "Look, there's Uncle Ed helping
Louise with her painting."
"Matt is playing in the dinosaur egg,"
giggles Tom. "And Dylan's yellow watering can is
just like Grandma and Grandad's. Let's go and help
them in their garden."

Grandma and Grandad grow things on their allotment.
"Look! Grandad's making another flowerpot," says Tom.
"And there's Sam and Arthur picking pumpkins."
"Let's help Grandma dig up the carrots," says Millie.
"I love digging!" Tom laughs. "Afterwards, can we go
and see the diggers at Auntie Bella's building site?"

"Phew, last stop!" gasps Tom. "There's Auntie
Bella, looking at the plans for the new house."
"Look," laughs Millie. "Harry has brought his mini
bulldozer, and Max and Sophie have their toy cranes!"

"Hmmm. Our family all love what they do,
but what is the perfect job for us?" wonders Tom.
"I know just where to find out . . ." says Millie.

"The library is full of ideas!" says Tom.
"There are so many other jobs we could do."

"But let's imagine the best job in the whole wide world . . ." smiles Millie.

"Working in a chocolate factory!"
shout Tom and Millie.

Find ten red stars to win these chocs!

Tom

Adam

Noah

Sarah

**Did you find
Tom and Millie's
friends in
the book?**

Toby

Poppy

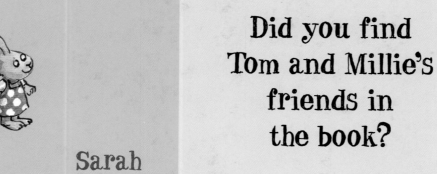
Florence

Jake

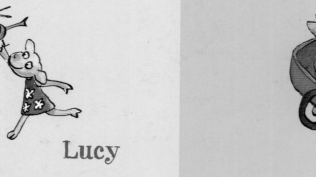
George

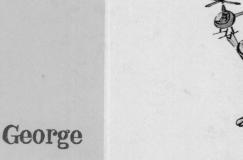
Lucy

Hannah

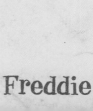
Freddie

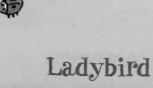
Ladybird

Olivia